Watcher

by
L. A. Weatherly

For my husband

First published in 2007 in Great Britain by
Barrington Stoke Ltd
18 Walker Street, Edinburgh, EH3 7LP

This edition published 2012

www.barringtonstoke.co.uk

ISBN: 978-1-78112-046-0

Printed in China by Leo

Contents

Chapter 1
The E-mail

Some people just have really bad luck. Maybe they're fat, or they've got spots. Maybe they've got no friends. Worst of all, there's no one they can blame. It's just the way things are.

Not me. I'm fat. I don't have any friends. But I know exactly who to blame.

My mum.

She'd been gone for more than seven years when I found the e-mails.

I was in my dad's room, on the computer. I was trying to log on as my dad. I was bored, and I wanted to go on the Internet. There are only a few sites my dad lets me go onto by myself, and they're all really stupid.

It was easy to break into his account. His password is *Sarah*. That's my name, and it wasn't hard to work that one out. But then, instead of going onto the Internet, I looked at his e-mails. I don't know why. He never gets anything interesting.

But I looked at them anyway. And I felt sick. I just sat and stared at the computer screen.

The last e-mail he'd sent was to *Ann Young*.

I started to shake. He'd sent it last night. He'd written to my mum just last night!

But *how*? We didn't know where she was. She'd just vanished one day when I was six years old. She'd left a note that said, *Sorry, but I'm not cut out for this*. She took all of her things. She didn't even say goodbye to me. At first my dad tried to find her. Then he gave up and told me that it was just the two of us from then on.

That's when my life started to go wrong. I put on loads of weight. The stuck-up cows at school all laughed at me. I hated everyone, and they hated me. Now, seven years later, I was still fat and I still didn't have any friends.

And now my father was sending my mum e-mails!

I clicked onto the e-mail. It said:

Ann,
I'm not asking you to step in and be her mum. But can't you just meet up with her? Or talk to her on the phone? She deserves some answers! You're living so close now that it seems silly for the two of you never to meet.

I felt cold all over. Mum was living nearby? Since when? Then I saw that she'd answered his e-mail. I quickly opened her reply:

Ted,
I only told you I'm in Milton in case you ever saw me. I don't want to meet up with Sarah, or talk to her. Don't ask me again. It's for the best.

For the best? My mouth dropped open, and then anger rushed through me. My mum was living only three miles away, in the next village, and she wouldn't even talk to me!

"Sarah?" I heard someone shout. It was my dad. He was just home from work. I shut down his e-mail. When he came into the room I was playing an online game, looking innocent.

"How was school?" he asked.

"Great," I said. School is never great, but it's a lot better than it used to be. I used to get called 'fat cow' and all sorts, until I fought back a few times. Now everyone just ignores me.

"Is everything OK?" asked Dad. He took his jacket off. He looked tired. He's the manager of a big supermarket, but I don't think he likes it very much.

"Fine," I told him. I didn't look up at him. Inside, I felt like shouting. Or crying. Or both.

My own mother didn't want to see me.

A spaceship floated past on the screen, and I blasted it. It exploded into a million pieces.

****

Milton is only a few minutes away on the bus. I went there that Saturday. It was a cold, sunny day in October. I wore my dad's old coat. It's the only coat I have that fits me, but it makes me look like a whale. I told myself I didn't care. At least it was warm.

I walked slowly up and down the streets of Milton. The houses all looked the same. I wasn't sure what I was looking for. I knew there wouldn't be a sign that said, *Sarah Young, your mum lives here!* But there had to be something. Some sort of clue.

After a while I felt out of breath. I'm not used to walking so much. The tops of my legs rubbed together through my jeans, and I felt like giving up.

Then I saw it. I stopped walking, and just stared.

There was a little bungalow on the corner of a street. The front garden was messy and overgrown. And there was an old red sports car parked in front of it.

My hands felt cold. I remembered that car, I was sure I did! I remembered sitting in the back seat and feeling scared because Mum was driving so fast. I remembered being sick all over the seats once. I thought Mum'd be cross with me, but she was really nice. She wiped the sick off my face with a cool cloth and gave me a kiss.

I went over and peered in the back window. I could tell it was the same car. The back seats were all cracked, and there was grey masking tape all over the cracks. I remembered the pattern. I used to think it was like a spider web.

I looked at the house. There were curtains on the front windows. It was the middle of the day but the curtains were shut. Maybe the person inside the house didn't want to see the sunlight.

Or maybe they didn't want anyone to see them.

I touched the car. The doors were locked. I looked back at the house again, and I felt sick. My mum was in there. I just knew it.

Part of me wanted to go and bang on her door and make her talk to me.

But then I thought of her e-mail.
I remembered what she'd written to Dad.
She didn't want anything to do with me.

I felt like I was going to explode. I had to do something! I put my hands into my coat pockets and felt my keys. I took them out. Did I dare?

I dragged the key across the door of my mum's car. It made a long scratch in the red paint. I made another scratch, and then another.

When I was finished, I turned around and went home. My heart was pounding hard. I'd never done anything like that in my life. But she deserved it.

Chapter 2
Waiting Game

The rest of that weekend, I waited for something to happen. I thought my mother'd ring my dad and tell him what I'd done. I was sure she'd know it was me. But nothing happened.

I was in a worse mood than normal when I got to school on Monday. I kept remembering things that I thought I'd forgotten. Like, when I was five I lost a doll that Mum gave me. It had been her doll when she was little. I was scared sick of telling her it was gone. I never knew when she might go mad about something.

I mean, really mad – throwing things and screaming.

But when I told her, she just laughed and bought me a new doll. It had curly dark hair and a frilly dress.

"There," she said. "That's miles better than the old one, isn't it?" So that was all right, then. But I felt sick and nervous, too. It was like waiting for the other shoe to drop. I remember that I had that feeling a lot when Mum was around. I never knew what to expect.

I had all those memories to think about, so I didn't feel like talking to anyone. But Beth Sands came up to me when I was standing in the lunch queue.

"Hi, Sarah," she said.

Beth is tiny. She's hardly even five feet tall. She has a thin, white face and limp fair hair. She doesn't have any friends either. But that didn't mean I wanted to talk to her.

I ignored her, but she acted like she didn't notice. She stood next to me in the queue like we were best mates. "I was thinking about our English project," she said.

"What about it?" I snapped. I held my plate out, and the dinner lady scooped sausage and chips onto it. The sausages were pink and greasy. The food's rubbish at our school.

"Well ..." Beth looked down at her feet and then up at me again. "We're supposed to write a story with someone, and I thought maybe you'd be my partner. It'd be really cool. We could meet up at my house to talk about ideas."

I stared at her. Was she mad? I carried my tray over to an empty table. Beth followed me.

"Well? What do you think?" She smiled, and I felt a burst of anger.

"No way," I said. "What would I want to be *your* partner for?"

Beth looked as if I'd slapped her. "I just thought ..."

"Leave me alone!" I shoved my face right up to hers. "I mean it," I said in a low voice. "Or you'll be sorry."

Beth walked quickly off, looking like she was going to cry. I ate lunch on my own. *I don't care if I've hurt her feelings*, I told myself. *She's a total loser. What would I want to be friends with her for?*

Dad wasn't there when I got home that afternoon. He works shifts, and a lot of times he's not home until late. Sometimes the house feels too silent, and then I have to switch on all the lights and turn the TV up loud.

I went straight into Dad's room and checked his e-mail again. There wasn't anything there. Mum still hadn't written to him about the scratches on her car.

Good. I stood up and turned off the computer. I'd got away with it, and now I could just forget about her. So what if she didn't want to be a part of my life? I didn't want her to be, either!

But as I did my homework I kept remembering more and more things. Like the way Mum used to hug me before I went to bed at night, and the perfume she always wore. I couldn't see my homework sheet properly any more. I wasn't *crying*. I just had something in my eye.

At last I went into the kitchen and grabbed a big bag of crisps. I ripped open the bag and shoved the crisps into my mouth in big, salty handfuls. I felt myself relax as I gulped them down. I know that's why I'm fat. It's because I eat so much. I can't help it. It makes me feel better.

When I'd finished the crisps, my stomach felt like it was going to burst. But I'd thought of a plan. I threw the bag in the bin and went and turned on Dad's computer again.

I logged onto Hotmail and opened a new e-mail account. I called it IM.WATCHING.U. Then I got my mum's e-mail address and I wrote her this:

YOU'RE NOT AS CLEVER AS YOU THINK YOU ARE. WE'RE WATCHING YOUR EVERY MOVE. YOU'RE GOING TO BE PUNISHED FOR WHAT YOU DID, AND IT'S GOING TO HURT! BE VERY, VERY AFRAID.

SIGNED,
AN ENEMY

The rest of that week I hurried home from school to check my e-mail. Sometimes I even checked it at lunch, from the computers in the library. My Hotmail mailbox was always empty. So after a few days I sent her another e-mail, even worse than the first one. Then another one after that.

I knew I could get into terrible trouble. I think there's even a law that says you shouldn't send threatening e-mails. The police could have arrested me if they found out what I was doing. But I couldn't seem to stop.

It didn't matter anyway. She never wrote back to me.

That Saturday, Dad had the day off for a change. He smiled at me as we ate breakfast. "Do you fancy going someplace, Sarah? We could take the train into London and make a day of it."

Normally I'd have been dead happy if Dad said he'd like to do something with me. Most of the time, on his days off, he's too tired, and just wants to watch telly. Most of the time he takes his days off when I'm at school. But going into London today was the last thing I wanted to do.

"Thanks anyway." I kept my head down as I ate so he couldn't see my face. "But I've already got plans."

"Really?" He looked surprised. "What are you going to do?"

I shrugged. "I'm meeting a friend of mine in town. Beth."

He was so glad to hear that I had a friend at last. He asked me a million questions about her. I told him all I knew, and made up the stuff I didn't. Beth and me, friends – ha, that was a laugh!

"Well, have fun," said Dad as I left the house later.

"I will," I said. I tried to sound cheerful. Once I got outside, I hurried to the bus stop. The bus was already waiting there, and I had to run. The doors closed just before I got to them. I banged on them with my hand.

"Please!" I shouted.

The doors opened again. "Come on then, love, shake a leg," said the driver. He looked grumpy.

I climbed up the stairs, breathing hard. The money clinked as I dropped the coins into the slot. "Milton, please."

Chapter 3
I'm Watching You

Mum's old red sports car was gone.

I stood in the road, looking at the place in the street where it had been. Had she even *noticed* the scratches? I pulled my coat around myself. The sun was out but even so, I was cold.

I hadn't had a plan. I just knew I needed to see my mum. I don't mean I wanted to *talk* to her. But I wanted to see her face again, because it had gone fuzzy in my mind. And I wanted her to see me, too. I wanted her to look out of her window and know who I was. She had to stop ignoring me.

My hands turned into fists as I stared at her bungalow. The weeds looked even worse this time. Her front garden was like a jungle. Without thinking, I started to walk towards the house.

"Are you looking for someone?" shouted a voice. I spun round. An old woman was standing in a doorway across the street. She watched me, her eyes narrow and mean.

"No," I shouted back. "It's OK, I don't need any help."

The woman took a step forward. "You don't live around here, do you? You get away from that house, now. Go on – go home."

Old biddy! I wanted to shout something back at her, but what if she rang the police? My heart thudded, and I turned and walked away.

There was a small park around the corner. I flopped down on an old wooden bench to catch my breath. Then I sat right up. I could watch Mum's street from here! I could see when she got back.

I crossed my arms over my chest. The sun went behind the clouds, and it got even colder. People hurried past. No one took any notice of me.

Hours went by. There was still no little red sports car. My stomach started to growl with hunger. Then it started to rain. Big, cold drops of water splashed onto me from the sky.

I'd had enough! I ran across the street to the corner shop and bought a Kit-Kat. I ate it in about two bites, and then I bought another one. I gulped that one down too, and stared out the window towards my mother's street.

My mobile went off, and I jumped. For a second I thought it might be Mum. Was she going to tell me to stop watching her? But that was daft. She didn't even have my number.

Dad's name came up on the mobile. I answered the call. "I just wanted to tell you to be home by five," he said. "I thought we'd go and pick up a pizza and a DVD."

No! How could I leave before Mum came back? To be home by five I'd have to catch the next bus. I bit my lip as I stared out at the road.

"Sarah?" said Dad. "Did you hear me?"

Damn, damn, damn! "Yes, OK," I told him. "I'll be home soon."

The next morning I was sitting on the park bench again.

I got there really early, but Mum's car was still gone. But this time I was better sorted and ready for the wait. I had Dad's MP3 player with me, and a bunch of sandwiches.

I ate them slowly, listening to the music. I wished Dad liked music that wasn't from before I was born. When I got fed up with the music, I played games with myself, trying to guess the colour of the next car to come down the street. Was it going to be blue, green, yellow?

I got them right sometimes. But even when the cars were red, they were never Mum's.

I sat there all day. The shadows under the trees grew short and then long again. Then, at last, it started getting dark, and I had to go home.

I stood up. I had been sitting for so long that my legs hurt. I was dying for the toilet. I walked slowly to the bus stop. I felt really down. Maybe she wasn't even there any more. Maybe my e-mails had scared her off and she'd moved.

The bus pulled up in front of me. The doors opened, and the driver nodded at me as I climbed on. "All right, love?" he said. He didn't look so grumpy this time.

I muttered hello to him as I paid. My cheeks were red. God, I was on this bus all the time now! How sad was that?

I sat down near the back, and gripped the seat in front of me as we pulled away from the kerb. Suddenly I felt angry at myself. What was I doing, riding back and forth on this stupid bus? My mum didn't care that I wanted to see her. She didn't even know!

I'd acted like such a nerd, hanging about her house. Well, I wouldn't any more. To hell with her.

I sat back in my seat and closed my eyes. I just wanted to block out everything – the whole world. Then the bus jerked and my eyes flew open – just in time to see an old red sports car as it vanished down a lane.

Chapter 4

Do You Want Something?

The car had been Mum's, I just knew it. Maybe she'd been away for the weekend or something. That was probably it, I thought. She'd been living it up with loads of her friends. They'd all gone off to somewhere exciting.

What if she went away every weekend? Then I'd never get to see her! I was helping Dad do the dishes, and I almost dropped one when I thought that.

"Careful," said Dad.

"Yeah, sorry." I stacked the plate with the others. My hands felt big and clumsy. I'd told myself that I'd never go back there, but I knew I would. I had to see her. I *had* to.

"Sarah ..." Dad started to say something, and stopped.

"What?" I picked at a bit of food left on a plate. He didn't say anything else, and I looked up. "What?" I asked again.

Dad shook his head. His hair looked thin on top, and was going grey at the sides. "Nothing," he said. "Forget it."

What had he been going to say? Something about Mum, maybe? Yeah, right! He hadn't even told me that she'd moved to Milton. I shoved the last plate onto the rack.

"I've got to finish my homework," I lied.

The next morning, I got dressed for school and said goodbye to Dad as always. But instead of walking to school, I caught the bus to Milton again. It was a different driver this time, thank God.

I kept my head down when we got there, and hoped no one would notice me as I walked along. Why does our uniform have to be bright green? It looked so stupid on me. I felt like the Jolly Green Giant.

Suddenly a car screeched around the corner. I looked up. The red sports car was gone almost before I'd seen it. But I'd had a look at the woman at the wheel. She had brown hair, like mine. And glasses. Mum had worn glasses.

It had been her!

I held my breath as I looked down the road. Maybe Mum had noticed me, too. Maybe she'd turn around and come back.

The sound of the car grew distant and faint. Then there was only silence. I stood there for a long time, but in the end I had to admit that she was gone.

What should I do now? I bit my lip. What if she'd gone to work? She wouldn't be back for hours and hours. But this might be my only chance. If Dad found out I'd skived off today there was no way I'd be able to skip school another time.

So I sat on the park bench again and waited. I sat there for what felt like years. I got so bored that I even started reading my English textbook. I hardly saw anyone at all – just a few people who were walking their dogs, and mums pushing prams. No one said anything to me.

After a bit I was dying for a wee again, only it was ten times worse than before. I started crossing and uncrossing my legs. Oh, God, what now? I hadn't seen a toilet anywhere. It got so bad that I waited until I couldn't see anyone, and then I ran behind some bushes. My face felt red and hot. I was so terrified that someone would see me squatting there with my big white bum. But it was such a relief to wee that I almost wanted to cry.

When I got back to the park bench, I stopped in my tracks.

The red sports car was parked in front of Mum's bungalow. I could see the scratches on the door. They looked long and ugly.

She was there.

My heart pounded. Slowly, I started walking towards the house. I didn't know what to do. Should I just go up and ring her bell? But what would I say to her? *Mum, why do you hate me so much?* I swallowed, and looked over at the house where the old lady lived. I didn't want her to come out and shout at me again.

Maybe I should go and look in my mum's window, and see what she was doing. Yeah. That was the best thing. Then I could work out if I wanted to talk to her or not.

I took a deep breath and started to go around the side of the house. Suddenly the front door opened. I stopped in my tracks.

My mum was standing there. It was her. Mum. She stared at me with a frown on her face. "Can I help you?"

My cheeks grew warm. "Um ... I ..."

She held onto the door with one hand. She was wearing an old denim skirt, and her hair was all messy. "Do you want something?" She sounded cross.

She didn't know who I was. It felt like the world had turned upside-down. I took a step backwards and nearly tripped over. Then I started to run.

I ran almost all the way to the bus stop. I could hardly breathe when I got there. I bent over, panting hard. Sweat ran down my face. I gasped, and then I knew I was crying. I wiped my eyes with my arm, and sat on the bench.

She didn't know me. She didn't even know me! I'd know her *anywhere*. She looked just the same. Suddenly I remembered this time when I was five, and Mum took me out to dance in the rain. The two of us had splashed in puddles together and we'd been singing as loud as we could. I thought she was the best mum in the world then.

It had almost made up for being scared of her.

The thought made me feel icy cold. But it was true. I had been scared of her. I hugged myself as I waited for the stupid bus to come. I'd never known when she was going to blow up at me. She'd get so angry sometimes, and I never knew what I'd done wrong.

Things were better now, with just me and Dad. Maybe he worked so much that I hardly ever saw him, but at least he never got cross unless he had a reason. Life made sense with Dad.

The bus came, and I climbed slowly onto it. I felt enormous – fatter than ever. *That was that*, I said to myself as I sat down. My mum didn't have a clue who I was, and I was glad. I never wanted to see her again.

Chapter 5
Reality TV

On the bus ride home, I started to feel hungry. I mean, really hungry! It got worse and worse, until my stomach felt like a big, empty hole. Food. I needed food. I was almost dizzy with hunger.

I almost ran off the bus when it got to my village. I headed straight for the chippy and bought three bags of chips. I felt better the moment I had them in my hands. I sat down on the kerb and started eating. I gulped the chips down in big, greasy handfuls. When I finished the first bag, I opened the second.

Kids in green uniforms started walking past. School must have just let out. Suddenly the chips seemed to stick in my throat. I hate it when people see me eating, because then they know what a greedy cow I am. But I'd never let *them* know how much I hate them seeing me. I kept my head up, and glared at anyone who looked at me.

Beth Sands was walking by herself. When she saw me, she stopped. She stood on the pavement for a moment, and then she walked towards me.

I couldn't believe it! I'd been about to take another bite of chips, and now I just sat there, holding them in my fingers. What was she up to?

Beth walked right past me, and into the chippy. I twisted around on the kerb to look in the shop. I watched her buy a bag of chips, and then she came out again and sat down beside me.

"Hi," she said. She opened up her bag of chips. She looked nervous. She should be!

"What do you want?" I snapped.

She nibbled at a chip. "I don't know. You looked lonely."

Lonely. What a freak. She didn't know anything about me. I rolled my paper bag shut. She'd messed everything up. I couldn't eat with *her* sitting there.

Beth turned to me. Her limp hair hung down the sides of her face. "You weren't in school today," she said.

"So?" I asked.

She shrugged. "Nothing. But ... are you OK? You look sort of – " she stopped.

"*What?*" I snarled.

She went pale. I thought she might run away, but she didn't. "You look like you've been crying," she said.

I jumped up. I wanted to throw the chips in her face, but I knew I'd want them when I got home. "Just piss off," I said. My voice shook. "Just leave me alone!"

I shoved the bag of chips in my pocket and started home. I didn't look over my shoulder.

But somehow I knew, if I did, Beth would still be sitting on the kerb, staring after me.

When I got home there was a phone message from the school, asking where I was. I deleted it. Thank God I'd got to it before Dad. He'd go mental.

He didn't get home until almost nine that night. We had a curry take-away, and watched one of those reality TV talent shows together. I ate a bag of chocolate biscuits while we watched. I was still hungry.

"Listen to him, poor lad," laughed Dad. "No talent at all!" He helped himself to a biscuit. He'd never said anything about how fat I was. Maybe he didn't notice. The thought made me angry, and I grabbed another biscuit.

"Why did Mum leave?" I asked suddenly. Dad almost choked on his biscuit. Good. It served him right.

He wiped his mouth. "Why do you want to know?"

I gave a shrug. "No reason."

Dad kept staring at me. Maybe he was trying to work out if I knew Mum was in the next village. I looked right back at him, and didn't give anything away.

At last he let out a long sigh. "I don't know, Sarah," he said. "I don't think she was always very happy. Sometimes she'd get really silent, and not talk to me for days. And then sometimes she seemed on top of the world."

He swallowed hard. "It was a real shock to me when she left," he said. "It was the last thing I expected. And it was very hard on you. You cried yourself to sleep every night for weeks and weeks."

I felt my cheeks grow hot. I scowled at the TV. I didn't want to talk about that part! I wanted to ask what she was doing in Milton. But then I'd have to tell Dad how I knew, and there was no way I could do that.

The next person came on the talent show. Dad kept watching me, like he wasn't sure what else to say. Then he turned the sound up and settled back onto the sofa.

Neither of us said anything else.

When the news came on, I crept into Dad's room. My heart beat hard as I turned on the computer. I had to see if Mum had written to my Hotmail account.

She hadn't. But she had written to Dad.

I looked at the e-mail on the screen. Dad hadn't read it yet. My hand felt like it was in slowmotion as I clicked onto it:

Ted,

I think Sarah's been stalking me. Someone scratched up my car last week, and I've been getting weird e-mails. At first I thought it was the locals in the village, ganging up on me and trying to make me move out. I can tell that none of them like me.

But there was a girl outside my house today, sneaking about. I asked her what she wanted, and she wouldn't say anything. I didn't know who she was ... but now I think it was Sarah.

Ted, you HAVE to tell her to stop this. She has to leave me alone! I can't take this sort of stress. I'll press charges if she damages anything else of mine, or sends any more e-mails.

Ann

Oh, my God! I quickly deleted the e-mail so that Dad would never see it. My hand was shaking. She knew it was me.

She knew, and she didn't care.

Anger rushed through me. I felt boiling hot, and then icy cold. So she wanted me to piss off and go away, did she? Well, she was in for a surprise, because that was the one thing I was never, ever going to do!

Tears ran down my face as I switched off the computer. Why was I crying? I wasn't sad, I was *angry*. I wiped my eyes with my sleeve and hurried across the corridor to my room. I slammed the door.

I threw myself on my bed and hugged a pillow. My tears dried up as I planned how to get back at her. Soon I knew just what I was going to do. I could hardly wait. She could throw me in prison if she wanted to. I didn't give a toss.

But she was going to be sorry.

Chapter 6
Mum's House

When Mum drove away in her red sports car the next morning, I was sitting in the park, waiting. She didn't see me. In fact, it looked like she was singing along with the radio as she drove past. She didn't have a care in the world.

Her car turned the corner, and I stood up. My fists were clenched. It was time.

First, I looked around the park until I found what I was searching for – a long, heavy stick. I swung it in my hand. It felt odd. I'd never done anything like this before. I couldn't believe that I was going to do it now.

But I was.

I hid the stick under my coat and headed for Mum's bungalow. My pulse raced as I went around the side of it. There were weeds everywhere, and bits of wood.

I walked round the corner to the back. A gate led into her garden. I tugged at it. It was locked, so I climbed over it. I was panting hard now. I almost fell as I dropped to the ground. God, I wasn't much good at this sort of thing! I heard a car drive past, and I froze. Nothing happened, and after a moment I relaxed again.

I walked over to the house. The back door was locked, of course. I took the stick out from under my coat and smashed in one of the panes of glass. Then I put my hand down inside. The key was still in the lock, and I turned it easily.

I opened the door and stepped into my mum's house. The broken glass crunched under my feet. The house was totally silent.

I could hear myself breathing. I gripped my stick in both hands and headed towards the lounge.

Thump!

What was that? I stopped in my tracks. My hands were cold and sweaty. Was there someone else in the house?

The noise came again. I felt dizzy with fear. Who was in there? Soft footsteps started heading towards me. I made a sound like a squeak, and lifted the stick over my head. I thought I was going to pass out.

A small ginger cat came into the kitchen. "Oh!" I gasped. I felt like an idiot! I put down my stick and leaned against the wall. My heart was thumping like I'd just climbed a mountain.

The cat meowed and patted at my shoe with its paw. It wasn't much older than a kitten. I picked it up. "You *scared* me," I scolded. The cat purred. I stroked its soft fur, and then put it down.

Right, I had to quit messing about. I thought of Mum, and what she'd done to me –

and I put down my stick and went into the lounge. The cat followed me, like he thought it was a game.

The lounge was nothing special. There was a sofa and a coffee table. Across the room were an armchair and a TV set. I lifted my stick up. I was breathing hard. What should I smash first? What would hurt her the most?

Then I saw what else was in the room.

It felt like someone had punched me in the stomach. I couldn't believe it. It couldn't be true. But it was.

Everywhere I looked, my face was looking back at me.

The photos were everywhere. On top of the TV, on the windowsill, on the coffee table. There were masses of them, and they were all of me. I dropped my stick and picked up the nearest one. It was me and Mum when I was about four years old. I had my arms around her neck, and we were both smiling. She looked young and pretty. Happy.

I felt numb. I picked up another picture. I was pulling pink paper off a birthday present.

In another one, I was making a funny face at the camera.

My legs felt weak. I sank down onto the sofa. Why? *Why?* She didn't want anything to do with me, so why did she have my picture everywhere? Suddenly I felt angry. How dare she keep my picture around like she was some sort of proper mum! She didn't have any right!

I'd smash them all. That would show her! I threw the photo of me and Mum onto the floor. I stood there with my foot over it. I was going to crush it with my heel, but I couldn't make myself stamp down. I just couldn't. I picked the photo up and threw it at the wall as hard as I could.

The stick lay on the floor. I kicked it across the room, and started to cry. I was so bloody useless! I might have known that I'd get here and then just chicken out. But I had to do *something*. I had to. I felt like I was on fire.

There was a thick marker pen on the table. I grabbed it up. I could smell the ink as I took off the lid. I wrote on the wall in great big letters, I'M GLAD YOU LEFT! The words looked scrawled and wonky. I threw the marker pen across the room.

"I am!" I shouted. "I'm glad! Do you hear me? Glad!"

I started to really cry then. My shoulders shook as I gasped and sobbed. I sank onto the sofa, hugging myself. I was so fat. I felt like such a freak. No wonder she'd left.

After a while, the cat crept out from under a chair and watched me. I felt bad that I'd scared it.

"Come here," I said. I put out my hand. It came slowly towards me, and then jumped up into my lap. I held onto it, stroking it.

I was so tired. I felt like I'd lived a million years in one morning. I wiped my eyes and sank back into the sofa. I'd just have a few minutes' rest, I told myself. Then I'd go home and never think about my mum again.

I must have fallen asleep. The next thing I knew, there was the sound of a door closing. My eyes flew open.

My mum was standing in front of me.

Chapter 7
Secrets

She stood staring at me like I was a ghost. She was holding a white plastic shopping bag, clutching it with both hands. I saw her read the big black words on the wall. She looked scared.

"Sarah?" she whispered, and looked back at me.

I sat up. I felt like I couldn't breathe. I wanted to run away, but I couldn't.

"It *was* you," she said. "Why have you been doing these things to me?"

My chin jerked up as I stared at her. Her hair was messy again, and her glasses looked dirty. "Why do you *think*?" I said. My voice trembled.

She shook her head. "I don't know. I've been asking myself ... I just don't understand ..." She sank down into the chair. The shopping bag fell open at her feet. I could see paintbrushes and pencils in it.

Was she really that clueless? "Because you left!" I cried. "And then you didn't write, or phone, or *anything*!"

Suddenly I was on my feet, shouting at her. "You left and I hate you for it! And then you came back again and you didn't even want to see me! I'm your daughter, you can't just ignore me!"

She seemed to get smaller with every word. "I wasn't ignoring you," she mumbled. "It was for the best."

"*The best?*" I opened my mouth and closed it again. I didn't know what to say. "It wasn't," I said at last. I was trying not to cry. "It was awful. You just left, and you didn't say why.

Then you came back, and it was like you did the same thing all over again!"

The cat had jumped off my lap when she came in, and now it rubbed against her legs. She picked it up and looked over at me again. "You've changed," she said.

I heard myself make a harsh noise, somewhere between a laugh and a sob. "Well, *duh*! People do change in seven years, don't they! If you'd been around, you'd have noticed!"

She gulped. Behind her glasses, her eyes were the same brown colour as mine. "Sarah, I couldn't be around. It was impossible."

"But *why*?" I cried.

I saw her swallow. "Because ... I know what it's like, growing up with that sort of mother. I was scared of what I might do."

I stared at her. "What do you mean?"

"I ..." She looked down at the cat on her lap. For a long time I thought she wasn't going to say anything else. Finally she said, "I was afraid I'd hurt you."

"Hurt me?" I didn't know what she meant at first.

She nodded. "*My* mother did, when I was growing up. She was always angry, always shouting. I never knew why. And then she'd be wonderful, and I never knew the reason for that. She got worse and worse, and then one day she attacked me. She had to go away for treatment. That kept happening to her, all the time I was a teenager. I was terrified of her."

My throat felt dry. I couldn't say anything. That was just like I'd felt, with her, when I was little.

She looked right at me. Her eyes were bright with tears. "I shouldn't have got married, Sarah. I shouldn't have had children. I'm just like her. One day I heard myself shouting at you ... I can't even remember why, now. But I remember how scared you looked. I wanted to hit you for it. I almost did. And I knew I couldn't trust myself any more. If I stayed, I'd hit you, or – or worse. That's why I left."

It felt like the world had crashed in on me. "So it was all my fault, then," I said. "You wouldn't have left if it wasn't for me!"

"No!" She put the cat on the chair and stood up. "It wasn't you. It was me. Sarah, I felt like I had a time bomb inside me! I heard voices inside me, telling me things ... I had to get out; I didn't want you to suffer the way I did."

"But you could have *explained*!" I yelled. Tears ran down my cheeks, and I swiped angrily at them. "You could have said something – kept in touch – "

She snorted. "What was I supposed to say? 'I'm as loony as my mum, so you're better off without me'?"

I felt cold with fear. "You're not loony," I whispered.

My mum smiled sadly. "Sarah, I spent over five years in a mental hospital."

Oh, my God! I thought. "But ... but you seem OK now," I stammered.

She ran her hands over her arms. "Yes, I'm better, but I don't ... I don't handle stress well. I start thinking all sorts of things. They seem so real to me, but ..."

She took a deep breath. "Anyway, I – I wouldn't be able to get a job, or anything like that. I'm on what's called an outpatient programme. That's the reason I'm in Milton – it's close to the hospital that runs it. They run an art programme ... art is supposed to be good for you." She tried to smile. She looked down at the plastic bag, and touched it with her foot. "I've been spending most of my time there."

Suddenly I felt almost sorry for her. She looked so small and alone. "Well, you – you must be getting better, right? Or else they wouldn't let you live here, or drive a car or anything. Or – or have a cat."

"I guess." She sat down again, like she was too tired to say anything else. The cat jumped to the floor and started to wash itself.

"Mum?" I moved closer to her, and touched her arm.

My mother looked startled. She put her hand over mine and squeezed it. Then she quickly let go. "I think – I think you should go now," she said.

"Can I come and see you again?" I blurted out. Where had that come from? I didn't know, but I knew that that was what I wanted. She hadn't been right to just leave us, but at least I sort of understood it now. I didn't want her to get away from me again.

Mum didn't answer. She looked at the words I'd written on her wall. **I'M GLAD YOU LEFT!**

"Are you sure you want to?" she said at last. "I'm not much of a prize, Sarah." She looked so small, sitting there in that chair.

"That's OK," I said. "I'm not much of a prize, either."

She really smiled then, for the first time since I'd seen her. It made her look young and pretty. "That's not true," she said. "And I don't deserve you, but if you really want to come and visit me sometimes ... then OK."

When I got off the bus that afternoon, I went to the chippy like last time. I bought a bag of chips and sat on the kerb eating them. Did Dad know that Mum had been in a mental hospital? I ate the chips slowly as I thought about it. I didn't think he did. He must have been just as confused as I was when she left. It must have been so awful for him.

School had let out, and kids were walking past. Some of them stared at me, but this time I didn't bother to glare back. They could think what they wanted. I didn't care any more.

Then I saw Beth walk by. She looked at me and quickly went on walking. I don't know why, but I waved to her. "Beth!" I shouted. "Come here!"

She came slowly over to me. "Hi," she said.

"Hi." I remembered how horrible I'd been to her. I wanted to say I was sorry, but I didn't know how. I held out the bag of chips. "Here," I said. "D'you want one?"

"Thanks." She sat down beside me and helped herself. She pushed back her limp blonde hair and gave me a shy grin. "You weren't in school again today."

"No." I looked down at the greasy bag of chips. I wanted to tell her the truth. "I was with my mum. She's – she's been ill."

"Oh," said Beth. She looked puzzled, but she didn't ask any questions. I was glad. I wanted to talk about it ... but not just yet. Anyway, I had to talk to Dad first. I needed to tell him what had happened – everything I'd done. There had been too many secrets between us.

I reached for another chip, and then I stopped. For some reason I wasn't very hungry. I closed the bag. I'd eat them later, maybe.

I looked over at Beth again. I started to ask her something, and then bit my lip. She might tell me to piss off. But I had to ask her anyway. I took a deep breath.

"Hey, Beth ... do you still want to be partners for that English project?"

She looked surprised. "I thought you didn't want to," she said.

My face went hot. "Look, um ... I was sort of a jerk before. I'm sorry, OK?" My voice sounded angry, but I wasn't. I just felt so stupid. But Beth didn't seem to notice that I had snapped at her.

"OK," she said. She smiled at me. "We'll be partners, then. I'd really like that."

I felt happy deep inside me, like it was my birthday. I grinned back at her. "Yeah," I said. "I'd like it, too."

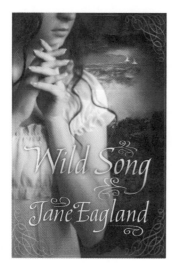

Wild Song
JANE EAGLAND

Anna's lived on the island all her life. She knows no one else, apart from her father, her father's assistant and two faithful servants. But one day, a strange boy is washed up on the shore. He's wild and free. And he has the power to change everything...

Tudor Rose
ANNE PERRY

When Rosie finds a very special watch in her schoolbag, four hundred years of history disappear to bring her face to face with Elizabeth I. A great Queen and a troubled school-girl find they can help each other in ways no one could have imagined...

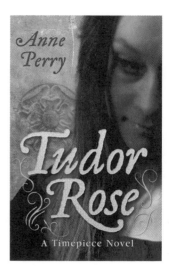

Crow Girl
KATE CANN

"She changed like Spiderman," someone yelped.

"Yeah! Bird Girl!"

"No. Crow Girl..."

Lily Stanfield is an outsider. Girls bully her, boys don't notice she's alive. But when she meets the crows in the Wakeless Woods, a new Lily is born...

Wasted
L. A. WEATHERLY

Luke's mum drinks too much. It looks like she needs booze more than she needs Luke. And Luke doesn't like it. Then one day, things get really bad. Luke has to escape, fast. Now he's on the streets, with no one to help him and nowhere to go. Can Luke save himself – and his mum?